STAR KA'AT WORLD

STAR KA'AT WORLD

ANDRE NORTON
and
DOROTHY MADLEE

illustrated by
JEAN JENKINS

WALKER AND COMPANY · NEW YORK

Text Copyright © 1978 by Andre Norton and Dorothy Madlee
Illustrations Copyright © 1978 by Jean Jenkins Loewer

First published in the United States of America
in 1978 by the Walker Publishing Company, Inc.

Published simultaneously in Canada by Fitzhenry
& Whiteside, Limited, Toronto

Trade ISBN: 0-8027-6300-6
Reinf. ISBN: 0-8027-6301-4

Library of Congress Catalog Card Number 77-79268

Printed in the United States of America

10 9 8 7 6 5 4 3 2 1

CONTENTS

1

Landing on Zimmorrah

A WIND blew the grasses so they bowed and rustled, while overhead hung a warm sun. But the sky—it was not blue with puffs of white clouds. No, it was instead faintly green. And those grasses which rustled and bowed were a very much darker green than Jim Evans had ever seen, with here and there a blade of bright yellow brown. Topping those were five-petaled flowers as pale as the sky.

The boy drew a deep, deep breath. This air was—different. There were smells he had known all his life that were not there. Others he had not sniffed before were. He looked around him warily. Those many small strange differences more and more crowded out the things he had always known, making him feel, for the first time since he left his home world, a little afraid.

A short distance away, Elly Mae Brown

threw wide her arms as if she would like to hug the grass and all of this strange world of Zimmorrah close to her.

"Jus' fine. No dirty buildings, no old smelly places. It's like Granny's place in the country!" she cried out with a soft laugh. "I do believe this here must be some sorta dream! I never no ways 'spected we would come to such a fine, fine place as this!"

"But—it's different," Jim protested uneasily. "You never saw green sky, did you? And look there," he pointed to one of the flowers, "or green flowers either. Now did you?"

"Maybe so, I didn't," Elly agreed. "Only I don't see why one world has got to be jus' like another. This here's Mer's world, an' Tiro's. And I think it's super!"

Jim turned his head a fraction to glance back at the small space shuttle from which they had just crawled into this new day. Tiro, his black coat shining to the last hair, and Mer with her drab grey and white, were watching the children intently from the open hatch. Tiro was not a cat (though Jim found it very hard not to think of him as such). Rather, he was a Ka'at, the descendent of a race—hundreds and hundreds of years old—of space explorers.

2

Jim, a little afraid of all this strangeness, felt a warm touch from Tiro's mind. "There is no need for worry, cubling. All is right for us —and for you."

He turned his head to look at the big black Ka'at, and Tiro's green eyes were friendly. Jim felt better. Sure, this could be a very strange world in many ways, but one would expect that. Tiro and Mer had promised to look after him and Elly Mae, and he was sure that they would.

Once, a very long time ago, Ka'ats had come to Jim and Elly's own planet Earth and found people there with whom they could talk mind to mind, so that Ka'at and human could exchange knowledge. Ka'ats came to live with the humans in temples and homes where they were treated with honor and respect.

Then—men had changed. There were wars, and during them the few who could "mind-talk" with the Ka'ats had been killed when their enemy looted the temples and the city. Ka'ats who still lived with men changed, too. They had had to, or they would have all died. They learned to hunt for their food, to fight, to kill—to be more like man and less like Ka'at. Ka'ats who still roamed space thought of Earth as a trap, a place of evil where there were always wars and bad things happening to man and animal alike.

A short time ago a new party had come into power among the Ka'ats. They had re-explored Earth and watched man foolishly poison his air, spoil the land, kill in wars. And they came to believe that it was right to rescue as many of their long-ago kin, the earth cats, as they could.

They had landed their small ferry ships all about Jim's world, hurrying because they were sure that man was heading for a last and terrible war. And from those ships they had sent out field scouts to locate those of Earth who still could receive the Ka'at mind-calls.

Tiro and Mer had been two of those scouts. Tiro had come to Jim because he needed a "home" where he might stay while he searched for those he would rescue. Just as Mer had chosen Elly Mae.

But then something very strange had happened, something the Ka'ats had not counted on. It had been so long since they could mind-talk with men that they did not even try very hard any more. But Jim had been able to pick up Tiro's name, and to know when the big

4

black cat was safe. And Elly Mae had been even easier for Mer to contact.

Perhaps it was because Jim had been so unhappy since his parents were killed in a plane crash, felt so alone in the foster home (even though the Dales had been good to him), that he could understand Tiro a little. And Elly Mae—she had been alone, too. When her Granny died she had no one but Mer.

It was Elly Mae, hunting for Mer through a bad storm at night, who had led Jim to the hidden space shuttle ship and had gone aboard, Jim with her. The other Ka'ats had wanted to make Jim and Elly leave, but when first Mer and then Tiro claimed the children their kin and agreed to accept responsibility for their actions, the children were allowed to go with the Ka'ats. So when one of the big rescue ships had swung out of orbit around the planet Earth, Jim and Elly were taken on board.

They could not remember the trip, of course. Since room and supplies on the ship had been so limited, not only the rescued half-kin cats but the boy and girl had slept away that time. Jim could not even remember any dreams. It seemed to him that just a little while ago he had been listening to Tiro explain where they were going and why. Then he woke up and crawled into the shuttle that had set them down right here.

He was not very good at mind-send even yet—not nearly as good as Elly Mae—though he tried hard. But he had picked up enough to know that this was Zimmorrah, the world from which Tiro and Mer came. It was not so different from his own that he and Elly could not breathe the same air or live here—even though many things looked strange.

Now Elly spoke. "They want us to go. There is another place for us," she pointed to Mer and Tiro. "We have to be there for awhile—with all the cats." Her forehead wrinkled in a small frown. "They think maybe we're going to dirty up their world if we don't."

"Dirty up their world?" Jim thought. He was not quite sure what that might mean. But already he was on his way back into the shuttle. Tiro's command had been a strong one. As he sat hunched on the padded floor of the control room he tried to think clearly, to push aside the uneasiness, the strangeness, of this world that had made him feel alone for a bad minute or two, in spite of Elly Mae and Tiro.

The shuttle gave one of those sudden

swoops that upset his stomach—like being on an elevator that moved too fast. Then he felt the slight bump as it grounded again.

This time when Tiro opened the lock they could hear a noise louder than any wind. There were such sounds of meows, rumbles, and even louder cat calls that Elly laughed as she crawled toward the hatch. She faced outward and then looked back over her shoulder at Jim, her eyes wide.

"I never saw so many cats in my whole born days!" she announced almost solemnly. "There must be hundreds."

Then she was gone through the lock and it was Jim's turn. He squeezed through the door and rose to his feet. Elly Mae had been quite right. He was standing in a sea of cats. There were all colors, all sizes, all kinds—Siamese, Persian, short hairs and some types he was sure he had never seen before because they looked so strange. There were mother cats with kittens gathered close to them, hissing to warn off strangers coming too close; half grown cats; thin cats and big plump ones.

Before them were some low buildings, or at least they looked low to Jim, though they were a reasonable size in the Ka'at world. Again the

7

difference in those buildings made the boy realize just how far they had come from all they had ever known before.

Into the nearer of the buildings the stream—or big river—of cats was moving; stationed at points along the outer edges of that crowd were the Ka'ats themselves. Though Jim could not pick up their mind-send, he was sure they were reassuring, directing the refugees forward.

There was a mother cat crouched close to where Elly Mae stood. She was a thin calico, her dingy fur looking as if she had not been a pet but had been lost and hungry back on earth. Now she had gathered nearly under her three kittens who were very young indeed, and she hissed angrily when any of the passing cats seemed to look at her.

Mer jumped lightly from the space shuttle and crossed deliberately to the calico, touching noses with the anxious mother. Then she stooped and picked up a black kitten by the nape of its neck so it hung in the air, its tiny paws wildly scrabbling. The mother took up a yellow one and Elly Mae scooped up the remaining kitten, a small grey and white.

"Come on!" she said to Jim. "They want the

cats and us to be clean, no fleas or bugs. And those who are hurt, they'll take care of them, too."

Fleas and bugs! Jim was a little indignant. He was perfectly clean—or was he? When he looked down he could see the mud stains on his shoes and jeans, dried out, but still there. And perhaps to the Ka'ats he was just plain dirty.

They had to get down on their hands and knees once more to creep through the door of the building. And inside—

Jim let out a startled squawk, which was not unlike the indignant protest of one of the largest cats. Because hands—no, not hands—closed on him with a firm pressure, though not with a squeeze hard enough to hurt.

He tried to pull away but could not. A metal thing, like a spider (at least it had as many arms as one, he thought confusedly), held him completely captive. A clawlike gadget caught in his tee shirt, stroked up and down it for a moment, and then deliberately produced sharp edges which had been folded away along the inner part and used those to cut him out of his clothes. Bare skinned, he was pushed into a small cubbyhole and a shutter door slammed

9

on him. Before he could protest, warm air, strange smelling, puffed up around his body.

It was like taking an air shower, he decided. More rods unfolded from the walls, each equipped with a soft pad which patted over his body and ruffled through his hair, sleeking it down, then blowing it up again.

After his first startled reaction, he was content to sit quietly and let the machine do its work, wondering what would happen when those pad things tried to loosen Elly Mae's tight braids. For he did not doubt she was having a similar experience.

There was another rush of air, cooler this time and with a different smell, which puffed about his body. Then the door of the cabinet snapped up and he took that as an invitation to crawl out.

The spiderlike machine was waiting for him. But it made no move this time to seize him; rather it extended one arm with a furry yellowish thing on it. At first Jim thought it was a towel, but when he shook it out he found he held a suit. It was sleeveless but as long as his knees, made of a thick furlike plush. He wriggled his way into it, finding that it expanded easily on his body and was so light in weight it

11

felt like another skin, not like anything he had worn before. It opened down the front and he could see no fastening. But, as if the spider machine could sense his bewilderment, the robot extended an arm once more and drew together the gaping edges, pressing them firmly together. They remained closed. And when Jim experimented a little he discovered that he could open his new clothing well enough with a sharp tug at the top and reclose it by pressing.

"Certainly beats zippers," he commented aloud when he was sure that unusual way of closing his suit would continue.

He looked about him. The flood of cats that had entered this building with him was gone. He did not even see Elly now.

Clearing his throat, Jim spoke again, "Elly—where are you?"

"Right here." She appeared at the other end of what seemed to be a narrow hall. Though there were marks on the walls along it which Jim thought might outline doors or smallish openings, they were now all firmly closed. He blinked.

Elly certainly had a new look. Her tightly braided hair was all loose and stood out in a

12

fluffy mass about her face as if it had been deliberately brushed to the end of each separate strand and then ordered to stand erect. Her thin arms and legs, hardly thicker than those of the spider machine, were as bare as his own, and she wore a suit similar to his, only of a different color—a deeper and richer yellow.

Now she smoothed her hand down her suit, almost lovingly.

"Jus' like fur, it seems," she commented. "Mer, she had 'em make these for us. Nice—so nice and soft."

"Had who make them?" Jim walked towards her.

"The work machines. They make everything—houses, flyers, whatever the Ka'ats want. You just sit and think at 'em about something you want bad and they make it. Come on—I'm hungry, ain't you?"

She caught him by the hand and pulled him on through another doorway where they had to stoop far down to enter. But once inside they could straighten up again. And here were cats in plenty each eating, with the steady concentration of the very hungry, out of a separate bowl. Jim peered into the nearest. The dark brown mess inside did not look too inviting, but when Elly Mae had said "hungry" it was just as if someone had pressed a button and his stomach immediately made him feel just how empty it was. He wondered how long it *had* been since he had eaten supper on that rainy night when he had slipped out to find Elly Mae and so got caught up in this adventure which still, at times, seemed so unreal.

Elly Mae passed the lines of eating cats, all of whom, Jim saw now, had fur as clean and bright looking as Tiro's. The girl reached the other end of the room and showed him two bowls which did not hold the mess he had seen in the cat plates. Rather in each was a kind of oddly shaped bun with bits of what could only be a hamburger projecting from it.

Jim scooped one up eagerly. "How did you get these?" he asked and took the first bite. It did not taste exactly like a hamburger, he thought, but on the other hand it was good, and he chewed eagerly.

"I told Mer—and she told the machine," Elly Mae answered proudly. "They don't have the kind of food we had—the machines make it somehow. Mer tried to tell me, but I guess I just don't know enough to understand," her smile faded a little. "I never got to go to school

14

'nough to know a lotta things. There was Granny an' I couldn't jus' leave her be, with no one to see to her. Mer says we'll go to school here—learn to think at the machines an' know how to run them."

Jim chewed and swallowed. A machine that made food—he supposed that could be true. It would be like Mrs. Dale baking cookies. Only she was a woman mixing up flour, eggs, and things, while this would be a machine doing it. And the Ka'ats—they didn't have hands like people—so they would have to use the machines as people used tools—to make things.

But—for the first time Jim's mind reached farther out—how had the Ka'ats made the original machines when they did not have hands to handle wrenches, screwdrivers and other tools? He did not believe you could *think* bolts into place or make metal without handling it somewhere, sometime. How *had* they been able to produce machines? Of course, he had read stories about making a robot that could then make another robot to make a third, and so on. There was sense in that. He could also believe that the Ka'ats might *think* the machines they now had into working for them and doing just what they wanted. Something like computers maybe—only all worked by thinking. But there had to be a start somewhere—and where did the first of all the machines come from? Maybe he could learn that in the school Elly Mae talked about.

They finished the hamburgers, which were not quite hamburgers, and then Jim suggested that Elly Mae try to get some ice cream—or maybe a Coke—

"Have to ask Mer." She was licking her fingers between words. "That's the machine—" Now she pointed to a square box of metal against the wall. And sure enough, Mer stood beside it watchfully. Elly Mae went over and stared into the blue eyes of the Ka'at. Jim moved his shoulders uncomfortably and the furry suit adjusted easily to his half shrug. There was so much to take in all at once. And—well, he still felt wary about this "thinking" business. He did not quite like the idea of any of the Ka'ats tuning into his mind—like he was a television set or something—even though it seemed to work.

Mer had turned her head toward the machine. There was a movement near floor level, and Elly Mae picked two of the food bowls out

16

of an open bin. She came back with her smile wide.

"Look here, boy, now that's somethin' to see!"

She set one of the bowls down before him and he saw a generous helping of what looked like either chocolate pudding or ice cream that had defrosted just a little too much.

"How do we eat this?" he asked. "No spoons—"

"Guess a machine what works for Ka'ats can't think up a spoon," returned Elly Mae cheerfully. "We've got our fingers an' tongues—let's use them." And she stuck two fingers into the bowl, bringing up a well-rounded glob, which she thrust into her mouth with very open pleasure.

2

The Evil City

"A HOUSE, a real house, an' all for our own selves! No leaky old roof to let in rain; no holes for rats like my old shack back home!" Elly Mae clapped her hands together.

She and Jim were watching the spiderlike work robots building. They were very fast and they seemed to know just what to do without any Ka'at to guide them. First, there had been a floor poured across smoothed bare ground—poured like cement. But the thick stuff hardened quicker than any cement Jim had ever seen. Now the team of robots was building walls, putting blocks of dull grey metal one on top of another. Funny thing about those blocks—if they were set so they matched just right, a minute later they couldn't be pulled apart no matter how hard someone tried.

Those walls rose fast, and there were other

blocks carefully set in at intervals through which one could see. Also, there was a door made taller than those of the other buildings, so that Jim and Elly Mae might walk, not crawl, in.

Mer, who with Tiro, had earlier brought the robots to build, came now and purred as she watched approvingly, rubbing her cheek against Elly's chin when the little girl picked her up. Tiro sauntered up a little later looking pleased with himself as he inspected the job. But he did not stay long. He exchanged a look with Mer that was probably an explanation for leaving that Jim could not pick up, and gave only a flick of an ear in Jim's direction as he left.

Jim drew a long breath. It seemed to him lately that Tiro was always going off on some mysterious business—at least it was mysterious to Jim. It was almost like the way kids back on Earth went off and left their pets. Were Jim and Elly Mae *pets*? He found that that idea did not suit him at all. He had believed they were *friends*.

The children had been on Zimmorrah three days and discovered there was always something new to watch. The half-kin cats from

19

Earth had been given quarters in buildings which had already been standing when the shuttle brought Jim and Elly Mae. And they seemed to spend a great deal of time gathered in small groups, staring, almost totally without blinking, at one of the Ka'ats who sat in the middle of each company. Jim knew that they were mind-talking, but it bothered him a little to pass one of those quiet, so absorbed groups. Though they never looked at him, he kept wondering if they were talking about him— him and Elly Mae.

Bad things had happened to some Earth cats in the past. Those might have good reason not to like people. What did they think about two people being here with them? And he and Elly were the only "people" on this whole world.

Elly bubbled over with happiness. She seemed to have no doubts at all that this was the most wonderful adventure, that this world was as beautiful as the place in the country her Granny had always talked about. But Jim could not help thinking—and worrying a little. Cat eyes were always on him and he had not seen Tiro for some time now. Only Mer was always there to "think" the food machine into producing when they were hungry. Some of

20

the things Elly had asked for tasted queer, but he had eaten them.

He was restless, too. And the couple of times he had tried to go away from the buildings one of the Ka'ats had appeared out of nowhere and had given him a very firm impression that he was supposed to stay where he was. He did not sleep too well at night. Perhaps the very long sleep aboard the ship had sort of rested him so much it was hard to be tired now. So he would lie on the piles of mats which were Ka'at beds, and think.

The robots both fascinated and bothered him. He had tried, and he knew Elly Mae had tried even harder, to "think" one of the busy machines into doing something he wanted. But not one of them ever paid any attention. Jim wondered what would happen if he was never able to get his own food. If only the Ka'ats could control the food machine they could keep both him and Elly here as prisoners—

"You look as if you jus' don't like this!" Elly's voice startled Jim out of his disturbing thoughts. "It's nice. Jus' the nicest house I ever did see!" She sounded a little angry with him. When Jim looked around he saw that her lower lip was thrust forward in a half-pout.

"It isn't really *our* house," he said slowly, wondering just how much of his uneasiness he dared share with Elly. She accepted everything as being all right, and had from the start.

"What do you mean? Mer told me this is a house just for us. They are building it bigger than the rest so we'll fit in it. Of course it's our own house!"

"But we aren't giving the orders to have it built, the Ka'ats are." Jim groped for the right words to share his feeling of not being a real part of anything. "We can't even get food unless Mer runs the food machine and you think to her about what we want. "We—" He motioned to those companies of cats, all intent upon learning what was now being impressed upon their minds. "Nobody is paying any attention to telling *us* anything."

"That's 'cause the real school hasn't started yet," Elly returned promptly. "We'll learn how to do things then, Mer promised."

Jim stirred unhappily. The robots had finished the walls of the house. Now four of them were engaged in the complicated action of fitting a dome for a roof. The dome came in sections, which they sealed together with expert skill.

The sun, which had been so bright that morning, was disappearing as banks of pale, greenish clouds gathered. A strong wind began to blow. The circles of cats and kittens were breaking up, padding back toward the other buildings, each group shepherded in by a Ka'at who appeared responsible for them.

A few large rain drops spattered down, making a loud pattering sound on the newly finished dome.

"Come on!" Elly urged him. "You goin' to stay out in a storm, or you comin' in our very own place?"

There was a clatter of metal. Spider robots crawled through the door, heading away toward the main buildings without a backward or sideward glance. Jim hurried for the doorway through which Elly had already disappeared.

He had expected it to be gloomy inside in spite of the windows, for the rain was falling fast, keeping up a real drumbeat on the roof above. But there seemed to be a light—dull and greenish, yet still a light—coming from the walls themselves. By that light Jim inspected the single room.

There were two raised platforms, one to the left against the wall, the other to the right. And on them were Ka'at sleep mats. Part of the far wall was covered with a glassy screen, completely dark in contrast to the glow of the other walls.

Elly Mae had opened a cupboard-like door and Jim recognized that the room inside was similar to the cramped cubbyhole to which the robots led him daily for the peculiar cleaning process that was natural here.

He could not find a food-making machine, so perhaps they were supposed to go over to the other building to eat.

The big glassy screen on the far wall now interested Jim the most. He went to run his hand over its slick surface. Not a window. Not like the food machines—then what was it?

"It's a learner!"

Jim swung around. Elly Mae was sitting crosslegged on her chosen bed place, and beside her—Mer. The girl's hand smoothed the fur of the Ka'at and her eyes were half closed. Almost as if *she* was a cat herself and was being stroked. Jim half expected to hear her purr.

"A learner?"

"We're dumb," Elly Mae said, as if that fact did not bother her at all. "The cublings, they know more when they are born than we do. It's how we think—all different. So we have to learn some things before we can even start in their school. That's how we're going to do it."

"How does it work?" Jim felt cross. Elly Mae always had an answer, and usually the right one, while sometimes he could not even make a guess.

"It works when you think at it—in the right way. But it's hard to learn that. We've got a lot of practicin' to do. See, this is Mer doin' it."

Jim jumped back from the big screen. It was no longer either blank or dark. Lines of color ran swiftly across it. Then those flowed together to form recognizable shapes. Recognizable, yet with an odd difference as if the forms shown there were slightly distorted.

What Jim was looking at was a scene back on Earth—the lot behind his foster home, full of rubbish that the men who had torn down an old house had not cleaned up fully. That was the very place where he had first met Tiro, Mer, and Elly. There was even that pile of old boards, the stiff weeds and rubble, and the cellar hole he and Elly had explored hoping to find trash she could sell for money to live on.

The boy had no more than made sure of that picture when the lines of color overran the screen again. This time he saw, not the scene from his old world, but rather the empty and fresh land he had viewed at their first touchdown on Zimmorrah.

From the screen Jim stared at Mer sitting so quietly, the tip of her tail folded over her paws. She wasn't looking at him or at Elly, but at the screen. They were seeing what she "thought."

So began their training. And Elly Mae had been more than right—it was hard, very hard to do. Sometimes Jim would sit on his bed place and pound his fists hard against the matting, sure that he would never be able to produce on that stretch of smooth surface anything but a jumble of random colors. His head would ache and his eyes would water and burn. Perhaps, had it not been for Elly, he might have given up. But she was straining at these lessons as hard as he was, and he was ashamed to let her think he could be a quitter.

Mer worked with Elly and Tiro came at intervals to aid Jim, although both Ka'ats gave only limited assistance and insisted that the children must learn to do this for themselves, that no one could open the mind doors but the one who had that mind.

Learning became an exhausting battle for Jim. And he was the more disheartened when Elly at last produced her first unaided picture. He had expected her to think out some part of their Earth past; but what she built up on the screen was the line of hills above the waving grass they had seen on that first brief look at this new world. He had been bitterly envious of her. However, that very envy spurred him on to greater efforts. He had stopped counting days—they went to eat, they slept in their bed places. But always Jim's mind was filled with the determination that *this* time he was going to do it, to prove to Elly, Mer, and Tiro that he could!

He was hardly aware that the circles of cats around their instructor Ka'ats had grown fewer each time he and Elly went over to eat. And the food did not have a strange taste anymore. Then he noticed that Elly's arms and legs were no longer so thin and her face had rounded.

Their fur suits were cleaned each day by some process known to the robots and returned, or others like them were produced, clean and fresh smelling. In addition, the children had now been furnished with foot coverings that extended well up their legs, made of a much thicker plush, and provided with soles that kept the small stones and gravel of the paths around the buildings from bruising their feet.

At last there did come the day when Jim produced his first unbroken and completely clear mind picture. It was dull enough—just the cluster of buildings around his house. But it was wholly his and he was able to hold it steady.

Having learned the basic study of the Ka'ats, Elly and he moved on to the next step of their training. And this was far more interesting.

"Field trips," Jim said to himself, remembering what seemed now another life, very far away and unimportant.

With a selection of both Ka'at cublings and certain of the refugee cats, the two children were loaded onto unusual machines which hovered some distance above the ground as they sped along.

With these they explored out, away from the

port town. And their lessons were different from any Jim had had before. It was necessary for him to watch carefully all along the way, taking note of everything that he could. Then when they returned, he was supposed to reproduce on a screen his memories of what he had seen. The smallest detail was demanded, and Jim began to realize soon that all his life he had looked at things without honestly, truthfully, *seeing* them. He had caught only the larger images his eyes had picked up, and had ignored many small, unusual details. Now he had to watch for leaves, insects, for anything that might be necessary to round out his "think" pictures.

And he learned, too, by watching the efforts of his companions, that minds all differed in seizing upon and retaining impressions. Some of them remembered points that their fellows had not seen at all. Elly, he soon discovered, had a dislike for certain bugs and when she thought them into being on the screen they were far larger and more ugly than he remembered them. On the other hand, her flowers and leaves were in beautiful detail, growing more and more noticeable each time she thought them.

Jim himself was interested in rocks; he

could not have said why. But he often brought back with him small colored ones that he sometimes arranged in patterns on the floor of their house. He wondered if some of these were jewels. Not diamonds or emeralds or ones like that, but perhaps others his world had not heard of. There was one he liked to hold up to the sun because it shaded from a deep pink to a creamy yellow and cupped light within it like a small lamp.

There were caves in the heights their carrier skimmed by. But the Ka'ats allowed no exploring on foot in the highlands. Rather, they took their students there to point out what must be avoided—a twisted plant that grew in great scallops up and down cliffs and that to Elly's horror, looped out a section of vine, much as a cowboy would throw a lasso, to catch a flying thing.

There were tracks they were also shown as a warning. "Look jus' like a big old chicken made those." Elly Mae had speculated. But the picture their Ka'at guardian sent into each mind was not of any chicken. It was of something so horrible Jim thought it might have jumped out of a nightmare. For the thing was like a toad and a lizard and maybe an alligator all mixed up together. Luckily, they were assured, there were not many of such monsters left. And the creatures never ventured far away from the disagreeable pools of dark, nasty-smelling water that their carrier had hovered over for only a very short time.

It was on their fifth voyage of discovery that Jim sensed a different kind of excitement among his furred companions. Several growled deep in their throats as if they scented or sensed some danger much worse then the toad-lizards. The Ka'at in charge radiated a thought of the need to be on extra guard. They were, Jim picked up, about to be shown—from a distance—what was the greatest danger Zimmorrah could produce. There was even some fear of their going on this trip at all, except that it was very necessary for them to be shown what they had to fear.

The flyer traveled higher than they usually flew, and sped at a faster than ordinary pace southward from the port buildings. The Ka'at in charge had closed her mind, leaving those with her to speculate about what lay before them. It was as if she was using all her force of thought to get them somewhere in safety—and back again.

They skimmed over a low range of hills that grew taller and taller, almost like a flight of giant stairs, until they merged into what looked to Jim like real mountains. He knew that neither he nor Elly shared the keenness of cat-Ka'at sight, and he wondered if they would approach the point of threatened danger close enough for the two of them to see it, too.

The flyer swept to the east after they were quite a bit out over the level country on the other side of the hills. There was a river running below and the children could sight brown lumps of heavy bodied grass-eaters browsing there. The Ka'ats ignored these creatures, dismissing them as beneath notice since they were, in Ka'at eyes, creatures of instinct only, possessing little intelligence.

Past that pasturage they went, but still beside the ribbon of the river. And then—

The flyer began to hover, poised nearly motionless over the water. Jim caught at Elly Mae's arm, his voice rising in startled surprise, "It's a city!"

They were still far away, but he was sure of the meaning of those high-reaching blocks. They were far too regular to be anything else but the result of work by some intelligent creature.

"A city—," he repeated. And he was sure that those buildings were not in the least like those the robots had built around the port. They were large, as large as those he knew from his home world.

"It is death!" The thought from the Ka'at mind fell like a blow. And he heard the audible snarl that accompanied that thought as the carrier turned and fled—for their retreating speed was like a flight—back the way they had come.

3

The Hsi Trap

"I TELL YOU it was a real city!" Jim said stubbornly. "And I don't think the Ka'ats made it, either. So maybe there *are* people, people like us here, too."

"Mer said it was dead," Elly Mae scowled. "Anyways, even if there are people, how come you want to go to 'em? If the Ka'ats think they're bad, then they've got to be."

Jim laced his fingers around one knee, drawing it up against his chest. No, he had not forgotten the sensation of fear and disgust their Ka'at guide had thought-sent to all of them as the flyer had fled fast and far from the distant sight of those towers. But he couldn't forget what he had seen in spite of all the warnings he had heard since. He wanted to know! A real city—who had built it? Were they still there? And why did the Ka'ats hate and fear it—or

35

perhaps its inhabitants, if there were any—so bitterly?

"Peace—" That thought slid into the muddle of his own unanswered questions. He turned his head quickly. Mer and Tiro both stood in the doorway. For once boldness got the better of Jim's caution.

"That *was* a city!" He repeated the same statement he had made to their Ka'at guide. "And—"

Tiro crossed the small room with the dignity of his Ka'at training. He sat down deliberately, Mer beside him. Both their backs were to the learning screen, but their eyes drew and held those of the children.

"The place," Tiro thought-sent with force and deliberation, "is a trap of death. Should any flyer approach too closely, that death reaches out and draws both Ka'at and machine to it, so that they are never to be seen again."

"But it is a *city*," Jim had spirit enough to insist. "Who lives there? People—like us?"

He shrank back on his mat. The answer to that last question had been a stab of chilling anger. And in that moment he realized just how vulverable he and Elly Mae were. This was a Ka'at world. *They* controlled the robots,

36

could mind link with each other. Suppose—suppose Mer would no longer operate the food machine; he and Elly could starve. Because, for all their trying, they had never been able to operate by mind-send any robot or tool the Ka'ats used with ease.

"You are like all of your kind," even a thought could seem very chill and forbidding when Tiro aimed it. "You reach out for the forbidden without thinking what might result from your act. Very well, you shall be told about the trap and those who built it, and Ka-ten who learned enough to make the Ka'ats understand what they could be—space rovers and masters of their own world and of others, too, in the course of time." Tiro paused, his green eyes half closing, as he thought the story into the children's minds.

"Long, very long ago, the Ka'ats were not as we now are, masters of Zimmorrah. But even then we were masters of ourselves, for by mind-send each of us knew the other's thoughts and desires. Thus, unlike 'men' as you call them, we could use logic to deal with one another and did not have to bare tooth and claw in useless battle to settle disagreements. We were not like the orrg who lies in the

37

swamp and hunts down the unwary, nor like the feathered ones, the scaled ones, or the grass-eaters who know only that they hunger and thirst and so must spend most of their life satisfying their appetites.

"But in that day we, too, had to be hunters so that we might live. Only we learned to work together and not against each other, not allowing greed to separate us.

"Then there were the Hsi—" Tiro's smooth flow of mind-send hesitated for a moment. "Since they also thought intelligently we could read their ideas at times, though that needed great effort on our part. But seemingly they could not touch ours. They were—" Jim thought that Tiro was now eyeing him critically "—they were not unlike you in their bodies and they possessed one gift that the Ka'ats had not been given. Their upper paws were formed like yours, having what you term 'fingers'. Thus they could grasp and hold, make objects obey their wills in a way we could not then hope to do.

"But they did not have the ability to mind-send; they were not open with each other. Even as your kind can conceal evil behind words and believe that his fellow will not know what he is really thinking, so did the Hsi. However, if they did not have mind-send, they had other ways of learning that they used.

"There were councils among the Ka'ats. Some wished no contact with the Hsi, fearing their unstable history, their sudden storms of emotion. Others believed that we must unite with them, at least until we could learn defenses against their superior use of tools. But even those mistrusted, and wisely, the Hsi ambitions. However, it was agreed that there must be a close watch kept on them, lest in trying to destroy each other (for they were like your Earth people, ever quarreling) they should also damage this world.

"Therefore, a choice was made of the most promising of the older cublings, those near full Ka'at skills. They were put in the way of the Hsi, who found them attractive and gave them homes with themselves as pets. But the Ka'ats were pledged not to reveal to any Hsi the secret that was ours—the opening of minds.

"The Hsi grew more powerful and their machines became more and more complex. There came a day when they took to the skies and then on into space. But always there was this flaw in them—that they could not truly communicate with one another and so their friendships never ran very deep.

"Ka-ten was of the third generation of cublings to live among the Hsi. And, though we did not know it then, he had developed a new type of interest that was not usual to our race. He was interested in the machines which labored for the Hsi, learning through the minds of those who attended them all he could.

"And unlike his kin he was different in another way, as well. He had a friend among the Hsi called Kindarth, who was of those sent into space on missions to discover what might lie among the stars. And Ka-ten voyaged so with this Hsi, sending us much information that was of the greatest service to us later when we ourselves took to space flight.

"He also discovered that Kindarth's mind was not altogether closed, that among the Hsi his friend was different because he possessed a measure of mind-send power. So Ka-ten deliberately worked to liberate that portion of Kindarth's half-closed mind. He hoped—because he knew Kindarth as nearly kin—that others like him might also be found among the Hsi so that we need not be so set against a closer relationship.

"On their last voyage they landed on a new world. There Kindarth was attacked by a creature that carried for its chief weapon a poison that slowly crept throughout the body. Though Ka-ten defended him as best he could, Kindarth was struck by the creature and knew that he would not live to see his planet again. But he would not leave Ka-ten on that savage world. In this the Hsi Kindarth was as one of *our* kind, thinking beyond his own hurt.

"So he crawled back to his ship. Once there he used all his power of mind to communicate with Ka-ten, giving him instruction on how to handle the robots that would guide the ship to its return. In doing this he broke the laws of the Hsi, for those who knew how to fly the star ships were sworn not to share with any—even their own people—this knowledge.

And Ka-ten learned. His mouth could not shape the speech which made many of the robots move, but he worked with Kindarth until he could reach those circuits within them that the robots themselves used as minds. And because Kindarth was a long time dying, Ka-ten had his chance to learn.

"After the Hsi died, Ka-ten took control of the ship. And he brought it home. But not to the field

41

where the Hsi forces waited. No, rather he landed it in a wilderness place and there summoned the Ka'at elders. They knew that what Ka-ten had done was a great deed, for the robots of the ship could be re-programmed by Ka-ten to make others of their kind to serve us, even as they served the Hsi.

"Because Ka-ten had hidden the ship so well, it was a long time before the Hsi discovered what had happened. To them the Ka'ats had been no different from the grass-eaters of the plains. Now they feared us. They could not understand and dared not admit that a Ka'at, a creature smaller and weaker in body, might be as the Hsi themselves, intelligent beings with minds that were greater and deeper in some ways than their own.

"A dark terror filled them and they killed our people, save those who were warned in time and escaped. And, not knowing Kindarth was dead, they spat upon his name and said he was a traitor to his kind.

"Madly, they began to kill Zimmorrah itself. Upon all growing things that might shelter a watching Ka'at they sprayed poisons that brought black and shriveling death. Animals

42

fled or died of starvation or the fire lances of the Hsi. For the Hsi had great fear that any living thing except themselves might harbor a powerful mind which they did not understand.

"Some Ka'ats remained in hiding, perfecting robots that would answer only to them. Others went forth in the ship Ka-ten had brought and sought other worlds on which they could establish peaceful colonies. But they took robots with them. Using these metal hands they could build, defend, make safe their new homes.

"The Hsi turned more and more to madness. They used poisons in the air and at last, one such escaped the control of those who had created it. Then Hsi died—in hundreds, and then in thousands. Until at last there was only one of their cities left on Zimmorrah. Into that fled their leaders, taking with them supplies enough to last for centuries. And they set up about it defenses which no Ka'at nor Ka'at robot could penetrate.

"But we did not care, for we had the new and exciting life Ka-ten had given us. We took to the stars. Many worlds knew the Ka'at—as yours did long, long ago. And our robots built better and more efficient machines and larger ships. Since

we were able to penetrate each others' thoughts, the greed and ill feelings of the Hsi did not trouble us.

"If any of them still live it is in that place of evil they built in the last days. We dare not go near it, for they have powers which can capture a flyer and draw it in. And around it on the ground is an invisible wall which no Ka'at can cross, though there is no reason why we should do so. This is the tale of your city, cubling. And it is not a good one—nor would I think you would want to see it closer."

"These Hsi—they were men?" Jim asked.

If a Ka'at could shrug, Tiro seemed to make that motion. "They had two arms, two legs, a head, a body not unlike your own," he answered indifferently, "and perhaps a mind like your kind."

"You don't know if any of the Hsi are still alive?" Jim wanted to know.

"It does not matter if they are. Though it has been so long a time I do not think even their children's children's children could be living. For near four hundred seasons our sentries have reported no signs of life. But the city lives—"

"How?" Jim wanted to know.

"Robots do not die," Tiro replied. "Robots were made to run the last city. Its defenses have not broken. And it is dangerous to any going too near. In the past, before we realized this, several flyers and all Ka'ats on board were lost, drawn into that city and unable to break free. We heard no more of our lost kin, nor were they ever seen again. Now it is forbidden to fly near it, but we show cublings this source of ancient evil as a warning."

Tiro rose to his feet, switching his tail. "You see there is good reason for all that is taught to you, cublings. The city is a place of darkness, of evil. It is the last lair of the Hsi and *it* lives still, even if they are at last dead. Do you understand?"

Elly Mae nodded vigorously, Jim a fraction later.

When the big Ka'at left, Jim stretched out on his sleep mat and closed his eyes, not to nap, but rather to think. That was quite a story Tiro had told them. It did explain one thing—just who had built the first robot. So the Ka'ats had, in a way, borrowed from the Hsi because they did not have hands to do the real work. It was plain Tiro thought very litttle of the Hsi and Ka-ten was considered a hero because he brought back that

47

ship and the knowledge on which his kin were able to build all they knew. But the Hsi *had* done it first. Even though their minds had been different! And the Hsi must have been men!

"The Ka'ats were sure smart," Elly Mae's comment broke through his own chain of thought. "Imagine one of them learning all that and then making the ship robots do what he wanted."

"But the ship really belonged to the man—" Jim pointed out.

"No, he gave it to Ka-ten—he wanted the Ka'ats to have it." Elly Mae corrected him swiftly. "I don't like those old Hsi—usin' poison, killin' things all over."

"They were afraid," Jim said slowly. "I guess people do a lot of things when they're afraid that they'd be ashamed of if they could sort of stand away a little and watch themselves doing it."

"Maybe so. But some of them ain't never ashamed of what they do." Elly Mae's voice sounded sharp. "Me, I know 'bout people like that. An' the Ka'ats didn't want to take them over—they were willin' to share."

Were they really? A small question shaped deep in Jim's mind. Elly Mae accepted the Ka'at thought power easily, as if it made a lot of sense to her and was all right. But, when Tiro was thinking at *him*, Jim somehow never saw a cat—Ka'at—but another person. Suppose you could not imagine him as that other person but only as a Ka'at and you thought that he was going to get at you, not scratching or biting, but in your mind. Jim's head moved on the mat. Why, thinking like that did make a person afraid! Sure, he could read pretty well now any message Tiro, or Mer, beamed straight at him. But what went on underneath those messages? It stood to reason that Ka'at thoughts weren't like people's. Jim did not see how they could be, really.

He believed he could understand a little of what had scared the Hsi so much that they went wild and tried to kill off everything. You—well, it took a lot of believing to think that you could talk without words and listen in turn to a cat, even if it was a Ka'at as impressive looking as Tiro.

4

Kitten Food

"I can't do it!" Jim pounded his fists on his knees as he squatted before the food machine. "I think, but it doesn't pick up from me at all!" He had been growing more and more uneasy during the past few days. The cublings and earth cats who had shared the instruction of the Ka'ats with Elly and him had no difficulty in mastering the right mind-send to activate any of the robots, beginning with the very necessary food machine.

"I can't neither," Elly Mae was frowning. "I jus' thought an' thought the way Mer said to do. But it's jus' a big old box for me an' nothin' comes out—'less Mer listens to me an' then tells it! Why?"

"Because," Jim answered, "we aren't Ka'ats or cats." He stared at the big machine. He was a little scared but he did not want Elly to guess that. What was going to happen if they could never learn to run the food box? Would the Ka'ats want to keep on doing things for them? It made Jim mad inside that he could not do what the youngest cubling seemed able to perform.

"Mer will help us," Elly said confidently.

"If she's here—"Jim had noticed that the number of Ka'ats at the port changed from day to day. And Tiro had been gone now for at least two days since he told them that long story about the Hsi city.

Some of the robots like those that cleaned clothes and the house did not have to be directed—or maybe they had been given permanent tasks. But the food machine was different—perhaps because with it one had to choose what one wanted to have.

He and Elly had both tried and tried to think out meals, but usually it meant that they just sat there getting hungrier and hungrier, while cats would push by them, stare at the box, and have a bowl slide out a short time later all ready. Jim had even tried to think "cat food" instead of people food. But it would not even answer them with that.

It made him wonder about the city. What would Hsi food be like? Something they could eat, maybe even like? If Ka'at robots would not answer their commands, might the Hsi ones?

Elly kicked one heel against the floor. "I'm hungry," she announced. "And I tried and tried to call Mer in my head. She isn't there—or here—"

"We can try another of the Ka'ats," Jim suggested, though somehow he did not want to do that, not if there was a chance to help themselves first. He knew without being told that the Ka'at teachers thought he and Elly were stupid. All the cublings the children had shared lessons with were now able to command the robots and had gone on to much harder studies. But he and Elly, they seemed to be stuck no matter how hard they tried.

But he was *not* stupid, Jim was sure of that, and neither was Elly. Look how she had managed all on her own back on Earth—hunting through rubbish to find things to sell and help out her Granny. Ka'ats thought all men were stupid because they could not work together well and had wars, and destroyed things—spoiled the country they lived in—like these Hsi had. But, after all, Ka'ats had had to learn from the Hsi and Jim thought that was not only because the Hsi had had tools and had known how to use them. It might have been true, too, that the Hsi minds could invent things the Ka'ats could not.

This machine was really only part of the Ka'at world because a Hsi had long ago shown a Ka'at how to make machines work. Were there Hsi still alive in that city? Jim wished they could go there—see—

He was shaken out of his thoughts by Elly suddenly getting up.

"There's Sitka, she'll work the machine for us." Before Jim could move Elly went to a big Ka'at who had just come in. He recognized the newcomer as the Ka'at who had taken them on a flyer twice to explore. She had orange-red fur and green eyes that seemed able to see any mistake one made. Jim frowned; to ask Sitka was shaming. Twice on their last trip she had thought-sent angry orders to Jim to pay closer attention.

Now there was impatience in the way she lashed her tail back and forth as she came to face the machines.

"This is the easiest of all thought-send," her scornful message reached them both. "Why you cannot do it—"

Jim tried to think quickly of one of the

rather odd hamburgers the machine could produce, and a glass of milk. But what slid out at Sitka's command was not in his mind at all. Rather it was a bowl of something that looked like a thin stew and smelled faintly fishy.

Elly accepted the bowl without question as a second one was pushed out holding the same distasteful mess. Then Sitka was already walking away, her mind closed to any message.

Elly held up the bowl as if it was a big cup and tasted the stuff. "It's what they give the kittens, the real little ones," she said doubtfully.

"I guess that's what they think we really are—a couple of kittens and real dumb ones at that!" exploded Jim. At that moment he wanted to throw that bowlful of mushy stuff straight at Sitka.

"Well, it isn't so bad—if you're hungry," Elly said. "I guess they are getting tired of us always asking for help."

Jim turned the bowl around in his hand, reluctant to dip his fingers into it. If he even had a spoon— He wished he had nerve enough just to pitch the whole thing out. But Elly was right; when you were hungry, good and hungry, you took what you could.

His nose wrinkled at the smell. Ka'ats and cats must have a different kind of nose if this was what they really thought was good. And it did not taste much better than it smelled. But since he did not know when they would get to eat again he made himself finish it to the last watery bit he drank from the bottom.

Unless Tiro and Mer came around they might find themselves in real trouble. He wondered if Elly guessed that, too, but somehow he was afraid to ask her. She might agree and then the future would seem darker than ever.

His stomach did not feel too good as they trailed back to their own house, and he thought gloomily that perhaps kitten food was never meant to nourish humans. Once inside he sat down on the sleep mat and faced Elly.

"Look here." He decided to let her know his worry; after all, it should be hers also. "What are we going to do if we're never able to work that machine? We have to eat and if the Ka'ats get tired of giving orders for us, then what?"

"Mer won't." But he thought that Elly did not sound too sure of that.

"Mer might not be here. She wasn't today.

And I haven't seen Tiro for two days now. Elly, we've got to try something else—"

"What?" the girl asked.

That was the very thing Jim was not prepared to answer—not yet. He countered with a question of his own.

"What would you do?" After all, Elly had had awfully hard times in the past and Jim was sure she knew something of what you could do when you got into a bad corner.

But this time Elly shook her head slowly. "If we were back home we could get us some throwaways and sell 'em and go to the store. But here there's no store—" Her voice trailed off and she looked troubled for the first time since she had lost her Granny and did not know where to go or whom to turn to.

"We just don't know enough about that thing," Jim scowled. "I wonder if even the Ka'ats really do. They use repair robots when something goes wrong, but you can't read robot thoughts."

He began to have an idea, a rather frightening one with a lot of 'ifs' in it. No use trying to control the food machine, or any of the robots. They had tried that too often and failed. And if Mer and Tiro did not return, they were sure not going to get much help from Ka'ats like Sitka. They needed more from the machine than fish stew meant for kittens.

"What about Pokadot?" he said. The calico cat with the three kittens had seemed to like Elly ever since she had carried the one kitten in on their arrival here. "Can you mind-talk with her?"

"A little. We make a lot of mistakes," Elly returned. "But she's real nice—nearly as nice as Mer. She lets me come and watch the kittens sometimes when she goes to class."

"Suppose," Jim began slowly, "you could put in Pokadot's mind some things we could get from the machine. "Not regular cat food. Maybe something like crackers, and cheese— or breakfast food, something that would last more than one meal. Do you think you could try that?"

"Yes. But why?"

"Why? Because we may need some supplies when Mer and Tiro aren't here. Does Pokadot know what crackers and cheese are?"

Elly nodded. "She likes them. A lady that had her a long time ago before she moved away used to give them to her sometimes. I saw her 'think' cheese once so the kittens could taste it. But only one of 'em ate it."

"All right. So let's make a list." Jim didn't have a notebook any more; but sometimes he wrote things down on some big yellowish leaves that dried out like sheets of paper, using a very thin stick to make the words. "Crackers, cheese. I don't suppose she'd know enough about chocolate or breakfast food to be able to tell the machine right. And not about fruit, either. But we could try luncheon meat—I bet she's eaten that sometimes—and maybe cooked chicken."

"She knows about green beans," put in Elly, leaning forward to watch the scratches Jim was making, "and corned beef."

"Okay, you go with her and see what she can remember of people food. Then early in the morning we go in there and she works the machine, gets us all she can. We'll need several days' supplies—"

"Several days?" echoed Elly. "You think Mer and Tiro are going to be away that long?"

"I'm not thinking about Mer and Tiro," Jim said. "I'm thinking of us and what may happen if we don't begin to make some plans on our own. The Ka'ats, they can really make us do anything they want to, because they know we have to eat. And we can't run their robots. Do you want them to think we're even more stupid than a kitten?" His cheeks were flushed as he folded the leaf list in half.

"But what—"

"We're getting out of here!" Jim told her. "We're going to that city. From all Tiro said, the Hsi were a lot like us. And he said they brought a lot of supplies there when they sealed themselves in. If we can find a way to feed ourselves—then we don't have to worry about Ka'ats deciding that they don't want such stupids around. You know that they didn't really want to take us from Earth. But Mer and Tiro, they said they would be responsible for us. Well, I don't see that it's very responsible to go off and leave us with nothing to eat. The rest of them couldn't care less what happens to us—that's what I am thinking!"

Elly Mae's face was very sober. "If Tiro and Mer get into trouble because we run away—" she began.

"Who's running away?" Jim countered. "We have to eat if we are going to stay alive, and I'm not sitting around here waiting for Sitka or one of the rest to give me a mess of stuff that makes my stomach ache, and think I'm dumb because my mind doesn't work the way theirs does. It's been a very long time since anyone has been in that city; Tiro said so himself. And probably all the Hsi are dead. But we don't know what they left there. And if their minds were more like ours, then maybe we can prove to the Ka'ats that we aren't so dumb after all. You can stay if you like, but I'm going to see what's in that city!"

Elly Mae pulled at her lower lip with thumb and forefinger. She looked unhappy.

"The Ka'ats say it's a bad place, a real bad place—"

"Sure they do. But they admit they've never been in it."

"Then how can we get in?" Elly Mae seized upon that eagerly as if she wanted to believe they were finished before they ever started.

"'Cause maybe we're more like the Hsi. Anyway, there's no harm in trying, is there? And we've got a good reason—we have to eat—and not this kind of slop either." He gave the empty bowl a push with his foot.

"I wish Mer was here—" Elly Mae appeared yet unconvinced.

"Well, she isn't," Jim retorted. "Now, can you get Pokadot—" He pushed the folded leaf into her unwilling hand. "And make as sure as you can she understands what we want and when."

"That city's a long way from here. How're we goin' to get to it?"

Jim grinned. "Well, I may be stupid about running the food machine and the robots, but I did look pretty carefully at the flyer—got Franko to sort of explain things to me last time we were out. Seems when the Ka'ats got the robots to build the flyer for them they just gave orders to duplicate ones they found in deserted Hsi places after the bad time, only with mind-send controls added. And so they have two kinds of controls—the 'think' ones that Ka'ats use and ones for hands, too—even if those have never been used. I am going to try them and see what happens."

"And suppose you can't fly?" persisted Elly Mae.

"Then we'll think about it some more." Jim hoped he spoke with confidence. Robots did not think for themselves; they performed exactly as they had been programmed. Copying the ancient flyer of the Hsi they must have duplicated every part exactly. And what Jim had seen suggested that the old controls could be used fairly easily by a being with hands.

He didn't sleep much that night. His plans all seemed simple and clear enough when he went over them again and again. But there were a lot of things that could go wrong. If Mer or Tiro showed up he knew that Elly would not only refuse to go but might even, without thinking, tell the Ka'ats everything Jim had planned. Also, he was not sure he could fly the aircraft, or if they reached the city, that they could get in. If the invisible wall about it was only set to repel the Ka'ats, they had a chance.

Ka'at flyers had been sucked in there and lost—Tiro had said that himself. But would the same defenses work against those who were not Ka'ats? Jim hoped not. So much of his planning was built on hope.

Before sunrise he woke Elly Mae in spite of her sleepy complaints. She went out to hunt Pokadot while Jim paced impatiently back and forth in the eating room, scowling at the machine.

Last night before it got too dark Jim had sneaked out and gotten into one of the parked flyers. For just a moment or two he had remembered—and his throat got all tight and hurt in a way he had almost forgotten that it could. Dad had flown a helicopter in Viet Nam carrying the wounded. And when he had come home again he sometimes visited a buddy who was a 'copter pilot for a big company. Twice Dad had taken Jim up for a ride, and Mr. Blackmer had shown him just how the controls worked. This Ka'at flyer was not exactly like the helicopter, of course, but he could see some things about the controls that were not too different. If he was real careful, somehow he was sure he could fly this. It would be risky, but by now the whole adventure was so important he could not back out. He *had* to prove he could do this at least as well as any Ka'at.

Now Pokadot trotted in beside Elly Mae; one of her kittens, the black one, followed to watch. After staring for several long moments into Elly's face, the calico cat faced the food machine. And the machine did come to life, shooting open the bottom shelf on which were things like misshapen crackers, and a big piece of cheese. Jim scooped them up to store away in a net he had taken from one of the gear rooms. Next, out came thick hunks that looked enough like cold beef, if one was not

63

too particular, and some more crackers. The third service was another lot of cheese (which Elly broke in half, giving one portion to Poka-dot), and some green sprouts, too large for beans maybe, but of the same general shape.

"That's all she can pick out of my mind," Elly announced. "And if we wait longer the night rovers will be coming in." For the Ka'ats shared this much with Earth cats—they preferred the night to the day for expeditions out into the world beyond the port.

"It'll have to do," Jim was hungry but he did not try to eat. He merely crammed the strange lot of supplies into the net. "Come on then!"

They scuttled, as might one of the spider robots, out of the building, passed behind their own house, and ended up where the small flyers were parked. Jim made no choice, only headed for the nearest one. He tumbled his net of supplies into the cockpit and helped Elly in. Then, taking a deep breath, he settled in front of the control panel. The seat made for a Ka'at was uncomfortable. But he forgot about that as he made a careful choice, pressed two buttons swiftly, and drew down a lever with almost too much speed and force, for the flyer leaped from the level ground with a bound that nearly sent both children flying out of the center section. It soared up and up as Jim frantically hammered on the lever, forcing it back to mid-point, and then pushed another button.

Higher than Ka'ats traveled they sped into the dawn while the wind whipped at them over the side shields with force enough to make Elly's eyes water. But Jim was filled with excitement—he had done it! Just as he had planned and hoped, he had brought the flyer to life with his own hands!

5

Into The Last City

JIM had no true guide, only his memory of the
direction they had taken on that day when the
sealed city had been shown to them as a warning. South, over the hills, and across a plain
where the grass-eaters spread out in herds,
then over the river. But at least he had gotten
them up without trouble and he could pilot
this thing in the direction he had chosen.

"It's going to rain, I think," Elly commented.

Jim only grunted, too intent on the controls
for any small talk, though one part of his mind
recorded her remark. The Ka'ats did not like
rain—their usual answer to a bad day was to
stay under cover. Jim realized now that they
knew very little about Ka'at life. What did they
do with their spare time? Often they all
seemed to disappear and only the Earth cats

were to be seen about the buildings at the port. They could not all be going off on their exploring ships. The large ones, like the one that had transported Jim and Elly here, were still sitting out on the landing field. And there were a lot of smaller ones there, too. He thought they were scout ships, able to carry only one or two of the Ka'ats on a star voyage.

The day was growing darker under the roofing of the clouds. Jim winced and Elly let out a small cry as they saw a flash of lightning flare fierce and bright across the sky. To fly through a storm boiling up that way was more than the boy wanted to try.

"There it is—the city!" Elly leaned forward in the small seat, made to comfortably accommodate a Ka'at but not her own larger body.

Against the wide sweep of the open grasslands the distant blot was even darker than the clouds. Only Jim's determination that they must not be always dependent on scornful Ka'ats kept him from hesitating. Instead he aimed the flyer straight for it.

Would whatever guards the Hsi had left be triggered by the flyer they were now in? The tales he had heard of Ka'at craft never being seen again were not just stories, he was sure. Was it the flyer, or the Ka'ats within it, that set off a Hsi defensive device? Jim hoped it was the latter, but he could not be sure.

"I'm going to set down." He hoped he could, but Elly must not know that he had any doubts about being able to do just what he said. "Then we can walk—"

There were winds pulling at them now. He had to fight with the controls and could only hope that he was not choosing the wrong levers. As the flyer was driven sideways, Elly gave another cry, but a smothered one. They were going down, though. These flyers were like copters back on Earth; they rose straight up, so they ought to be able to set down in the same fashion.

Jim eased back the lever that had taken them aloft, doing it very slowly, not wanting to plow into the field below with force enough to perhaps knock them both out. Though the wind was still battering them westward, they *were* coming down.

Then there came a bump that would have thrown Jim out of his seat if he had not been belted in. They were down! Actually, really down just as the storm broke with huge rain-drops that became a drenching curtain in a matter of seconds!

Jim tugged at the buckle of his seat belt and grabbed behind him for their packet of supplies.

"Come on! Maybe if we run for it—"

He scrambled from the flyer. For a long moment it seemed that Elly Mae was not going to follow. Then she climbed out, shivering, shaking every time the lightning hit and the thunder rolled. Jim seized her by one hand. He had not dared get too near to the city for fear of whatever pulled in the Ka'at flyers. But to him the taller buildings standing there had for a moment or two the familiar look of Earth, and that heartened him.

They ran through the storm, the water pelting them, soaking through their fur-plush suits, plastering their hair to their skulls, beating at them.

And as they came closer and closer, the buildings stood higher. Unlike the squat ones around the Ka'at port, these were several stories tall, even on the outer rim of the one-time city. In spite of the rain Jim could make out ever larger ones looming ahead. Then they

70

came abruptly to a strip of ground where the tall grass ceased to grow. Beyond was bare soil that extended up to the walls of the nearest buildings.

Elly pulled back against Jim's hold. "It don't look right—"

He caught her protest only faintly because of the noise the storm was making.

"Come on!" He ran forward, dragging the girl behind him.

There was a queer feeling as if something he couldn't see was trying to stop him. His skin prickled all over and he felt a sudden sharp pain through his head. But he kept on doggedly. They wavered across the space of bald ground and came to the first wall.

There was not a single window or opening he could see and the building was a long one. But turning to the right Jim headed to the end of the one they had faced. And he had been right, for before the next structure arose there was an open space between. Into that he moved, having to give Elly's arm a hard jerk to bring her with him.

They were in a slit of alley that ran inward between two of the buildings. Ahead, shadows were so thick Jim could not see the end of this way. But there was something else. The minute they had entered this passage, they were out of the storm.

He looked back. The rain was just as heavy over the land they had just crossed, making so thick a curtain he could hardly see the flyer. But here they were in the dry, even though, when he leaned his head back on his shoulders and looked as far up as he could, Jim saw no roof above.

The buildings on either side were smooth unbroken walls of a uniform shade of dull grey, like huge boxes. Under their feet there was a pavement of the same material, as clear of any dust as if it had been swept only moments earlier.

Elly pulled free from his hold. "I don't like this place. It—it looks like a jailhouse!"

Jim felt the same way but he was not going to admit it. "We got in, didn't we? And the Ka'ats can't. Now we just have to explore." But as he started down that narrow dark slit of an alley, Elly just a little behind, he was frightened, yes. It was as if something knew they were there, was just waiting to—

No! To think like that was a good way to bring on trouble. Dad had said any troubles

72

you imagined never turned out to be as bad as you believed they were going to be. As Dad had said—Jim swallowed twice very fast. He wished Dad and Mom were here. No, he wished everything was like it was at home before the plane crash—

Wishing was not going to make that so, either. Just he and Elly were here—and nothing alarming had appeared yet to threaten them. He walked a little faster. The soft soles of the boots the Ka'ats had furnished them did not click as they stepped out, but they did make a kind of whispering sound no matter how hard Jim tried to walk softly.

He glanced at Elly. She was staring straight ahead, her eyes looking too large for her face, her head turning a little this way and that at every step as if she was afraid to see something but even more afraid that it might come before she saw it. And he felt the same way.

The alley came out on a larger street with curves. And here they could see that the buildings, though they did not have any windows, did have doors. There was no color but the dull gray, and each building was exactly like the next, even to the fact that every one of those doors was tightly shut.

Daring mainly because his fear forced him to be, Jim went to the nearest of those doors. There was no knob. He pushed hard against the surface with the palm of his hand, only to find it immovable. Maybe he should pound against it, let anyone inside know. But Jim could not bring himself to do that.

It was so quiet—so—so deserted. Elly Mae stood in the center of the street. She had a fist up, hiding her mouth as if she were trying to hold back a scream. Her eyes were wide with fright such as Jim had never seen in them before.

"I want to go back!" she half whispered around her fist. "I want to go away from this here place!"

"We can't," Jim summoned all his courage to say that. "We have to find out about the food, remember?"

But Elly shook her head. "Better eat kitten stuff than stay here."

Her words added to Jim's fear and to his anger for being afraid. No, he was not going to go running back to the port just because a door wouldn't open! They couldn't leave now, they just couldn't!

74

He started on along the curve of the street. In spite of the gloom he could see another one of those narrow openings between the blocks of houses—if these were houses—up ahead that ought to take them farther in. And he believed if there were any storehouses such as he imagined, they would be a lot closer to the center of the city.

He looked back once. Elly Mae, her face screwed up in a scowl, was following him. Maybe she was afraid to try to leave the city all by herself. But she came so slowly and reluctantly Jim had to stop at the opening of the alley to wait for her. He himself did not want to turn into that even darker way alone.

Were all the Hsi dead? He began to think so. But their city seemed strong enough. None of the buildings was crumbled looking. Of course, there were no windows to be smashed, but every door was closed. As if whoever had once lived here had just packed up and gone away and left it—

They were in the second alley, nearly down to a lighter space ahead, when they heard the noise and stopped instantly. It was a thumping, Jim decided, not like the sound of feet at all—and it came from ahead. For some reason the noise, strange as it was, made him feel less afraid.

But he kept close to the right wall of the alley, Elly behind him again, and took very cautious steps. Then they were looking out upon the curve of another street, wider this time and with taller buildings on it.

"Look!"

Jim did not need Elly's clutch on his shoulder, her pointing finger; he had already sighted what was moving along to their left, about to turn around the curve.

It was not one of the scuttling spiderlike robots of the Ka'ats— No, this moving mass of metal was far more compact. And—it was cleaning the street!

A robot street cleaner! That must mean that someone wanted to keep the city going— Perhaps if they followed it—at a safe distance, of course—they could find whoever had started it on its job.

But when Jim would have put that plan to the test, Elly clutched at him desperately. And a moment later the now distant *thump-thump* of the cleaner was swallowed up by something much less innocent sounding.

This sounded like footsteps, a clink of metal against metal. Jim shrank back into the mouth of the alley. He crouched in the darkest pool of shadow he could find, shoulder to shoulder with Elly, whose hands were over her mouth now as if she could so muffle all sound of her breathing.

From their left moved another figure, about as tall, Jim thought, as his Dad had been. Hsi—? But no, this was metal, too. Yet it had been made to look almost like a man—there were two legs, now stolidly pacing along, an egg-shaped body with the larger portion to the top, and that was surmounted by a conical head. Folded against the body were what looked like two pairs of arms, each set ending in claws, those of the upper arms much the smaller. Around the head, which showed no indication of mouth or ears, there was a complete circle of disks. Each was about the size of Jim's own thumb and flashed off and on in a glittering pattern.

If those were eyes, at least it did not see the children. Rather, it kept purposefully on its way after the sweeper. But Jim could guess that it was a far more complex machine than the other, perhaps even a guard walking a sen-

try beat here. And he did not in the least like the look of those claws, either large or small.

They waited until the robot was entirely out of sight around the curve before they dared move.

"That ain't goin' to catch me!" Elly declared. "I'm goin' back!"

Perhaps she was right, Jim had to admit. He was shaken by what he had seen. To be the prisoner of that metal monster—it was a nightmare.

"All right," he gave in. Elly had already started down the alley again.

Then, all at once, she gave a cry and would have fallen if her shoulder had not scraped against the wall. She had both hands over her ears and her eyes were screwed up tightly.

"No! No!"

Perhaps less clearly than Elly, Jim had caught that same signal—Tiro! Tiro mind-sending clear and sharp.

"Mer and Tiro—!" Elly shivered. "No!"

But it must be true. No Ka'at would have sent a message like that if it were not. A flyer coming too near the mysterious boundaries of the city—being pulled in—and on board, Mer and Tiro.

Elly's eyes opened. "They—they must have been huntin' us! Now—that clawed thing is goin' to get them. We mustn't let it! We can't—" She stood away from the wall and began to run. Not away from the street where they had seen the robots pass, but into it and down it. Jim, the bundle of food bumping against him as he picked up speed, pounded after her.

The street curved and kept on curving. Jim began to believe that all the streets here were really big circles, connected one to another by the narrow alleys—something like the web of a huge spider. He drew level with Elly.

"Listen," he panted, "we can't just go charging in this way. We could be picked up by that thing before we could do any good. We've got to keep free if we're going to help—"

He feared Elly was beyond listening. Where Mer was concerned she was hard to handle. But now she glanced at him.

"I suppose you're right," she admitted angrily. "But we've got to help them."

"We will," Jim promised, wondering just how slender a promise that was and if he had the least chance of keeping it. But the boy agreed with Elly on one point. If Mer and Tiro were somewhere in this pile, then they had to be helped.

"Do no good to just run this way," he panted. "Better head into the center of the city. Seems they would have the main buildings there."

Elly slowed. They were again near the mouth of one of those connecting alleys. "Guess that makes sense. All right, let's go!"

They sped down the alley to find another curved road, again with silent door-barred buildings flanking it. And another alley ahead. This one seemed shorter to Jim.

Elly kept a step or so ahead of him. Now she turned to speak over her shoulder. "They got them—Mer and Tiro—"

Jim used his own hard won mind-talk—Tiro, yes. But the Ka'at did not seem aware of Jim at all. He was instead a seething fury of rage mixed with fear.

"I can find Mer," Elly said confidently. "But she's afraid—so afraid. I never knew Mer could be afraid—" Her face was very troubled.

They had come to the end of the last alley; before them lay the center of the web city. There were four buildings much taller than any they had seen before; and in the midst of those a fifth towered well up into the dull dark sky.

But the open space immediately before them was occupied, the last inner street encircling this heart core had its people.

6

Into the Tower

THIS CROWD was not of real people but of those metal things that walked on two legs. Some had their upper arms folded tightly against them, like the first one the children had seen earlier. Others allowed the arms to dangle free. Some held them out a little way and clashed the claws open and shut, making a noise that brought shivers to Jim. Elly Mae crowded closer to him.

"They—they's goin' to get us," she said in a whisper so small he could barely hear. Jim, though, after a long minute of watching, sensed that there was something strange about the walking robots. These were machines. Oh, yes, they walked around like men. And he did not doubt that they were dangerous; he certainly did not like the look of those claws opening and shutting. But they were not real people.

However, people had planned them, made them. And that meant that once they had done just what people had told them to.

Jim crouched down and pulled the shivering Elly beside him. "Watch them," he ordered. "Do you see anything out there—any one— that looks *real?*"

"What do you mean, real?" she demanded. "They's real—too real!"

"I mean people—like us."

He had been watching as carefully as he could while the robots paraded around and around the buildings before them. Trouble was that the machines looked so much alike it was hard to tell one from the next. The only differ- ence seemed to be that some waved their claws or their arms about, and the other kept them closer to their bodies, folded down. But nowhere had Jim seen any real person.

"I ain't seen none no how," Elly whispered. "Jim—" Her fingers tightened on his upper arm with strength enough to bruise it. "Mer—Tiro—they're 'way in there—in that big middle part, I think."

Jim, too, had picked up the signal. Not a signal really because it had carried no message—just a feeling of fear, fear so strong that he jerked as his mind picked it up. Somehow the thought hurt more than Elly's hand hold.

"Yes," he agreed. "They're in there. And we've got to get to them."

Only to do that meant getting through that mob of robots continually trudging around and around the open way between the children and the nearest building. Jim believed that the metal creatures were on guard. So could he and Elly get by them?

People—if the Hsi *had* been people—had made these things and set them on patrol. On guard—against Ka'ats? As Jim considered this, he caught a coherent thought which was not of his own for the first time.

"Tiro!" Maybe he even repeated that name aloud. Then, quickly as he could, he answered with the mind-send that was still so strange and difficult for him to use.

"Tiro, where are you?"

"Go—go!" The command was delivered with force enough to make a pain in Jim's head.

"No!" the boy answered. "Tiro—are there Hsi? Have you seen any?"

"The Hsi are dead—long dead. Only their evil servants live." Tiro seemed to have his own fear under control now.

Jim considered what the Ka'at had reported. He was sure that Tiro would have been able to pick up traces of Hsi thinking, just as the scout had been able to use his talent back on Jim's own world, not only to establish a tie with Jim, but to learn other things, as well.

Jim licked his lips. So the Hsi were dead. But these— He tried to remember the scraps he had read about computers, about robots. Most of his information had come from made-up stories. But he also knew that some of the made-up things had later come true. Look at that writer called Verne who had written all about submarines more than a hundred years ago, when everyone believed that such things would never exist at all. And the atom bomb, and the atom engines—those had been in stories, too.

So, suppose you could start a computer, build robots like these. Men might die and all be gone, but the machines would keep on working, just doing what they were programmed last to do. The robots out there, maybe they had been programmed to be guards. So

88

they just kept on being guards. Even when it did not mean anything anymore, like the street sweeper that kept on cleaning even if there were no longer any Hsi to care whether the streets were clean or dusty.

But if the robots had been set against Ka'ats as the Ka'ats said, what would they do to Jim if he just walked out there?

The boy caught his lower lip between his teeth and bit on it hard. He did not want to try it—those clashing claws—the swinging arms— No, he did not want to go out there. But somehow he would have to sooner or later, he knew that. If he just turned and ran away now—! Dad had always said if you have something tough to do the best thing is to go and do it, get it out of the way.

Jim dropped his small pack and got to his feet.

"What you goin' to do?" He had almost forgotten about Elly Mae, but she was here. Now he had to think about her.

"When I go out there," he told her, "you just cut and run. Run as hard as you can—get out of this place."

In the gloom he saw her head shake violently from side to side.

"Ain't goin' to! Mer's here. I ain't runnin' away an' leavin' Mer, not for nothin' in this whole world! So there, boy!"

Her anger was fierce, though Jim did not know if it was now turned against him or against the parading robots.

"You got to stay here then." The boy met her stubbornness with his own. He did not want to have to worry about what was going to happen to Elly if those robots didn't like Earth people any more than Ka'ats. He could run fast. Heck, he'd won the dash two years straight at school. He could make it, maybe, right through those marching robots. They were stiff and they did not move too fast. That much he had learned from watching them even this short a time. But he was not going to try pulling Elly Mae along with him on any such dash.

"I can run just as good as you." She was on her feet now, too, her hands balled into fists and held close to either side of her thin chest. "And we don't try it too close together. Maybe we can sort of mix them up that way if they try to catch us. See," now she pointed, "I'll head towards that place there. You go to the side of the other building. Mer and Tiro—they're in the big middle one somewheres."

Jim shrugged. He knew better than to argue with Elly Mae when she wore that look. Darn! She could just blow the whole thing, but they would have to do it her way.

They hesitated a moment more, watching the robots that never varied their swing back and around. Then Jim took off, wasting no time or attention on Elly Mae. He went with a leap and began to dodge in and out among the marching robots, expecting every moment to feel the pinch of a claw holding him prisoner. But to the guards it was as if he was invisible. Not one of them appeared to really look at him (if robots *could* look). And certainly not one claw had grabbed at him.

Panting, he nearly ran into the wall of the building. Then he turned to look for Elly. Something moved against the building just a narrow space away—Elly. So they had both been pretty lucky. Also, Jim felt a little braver and glad that he had been able to prove something that might help them later. The marching robots paid no attention to them at all. Did they look so much like the long gone Hsi that the robots believed the children to be their old masters?

At least in the much narrower space between this building and the far taller middle one there was nothing moving. However, Jim thought it wiser to circle around. Also they would have to find an open door into that center structure, and the only one he could see from here was closed.

He waved an arm towards the girl, beckoning her to join him. With the outer circle of the buildings between them and the still constant *clink-clank* of the marching robots, they slipped over to the central building and began to follow its wall. Unlike the others they had seen and passed in this strange city, this building was circular, pointing into the sky, Jim thought, rather like a warning finger, a giant's finger. It even grew thinner and thinner the higher it went, the way a finger was shaped.

They must have been halfway around it when Elly cried out, "Look!"

Parked in the space between the tower and the outer buildings was one of the Ka'ats' flyers.

"Mer's—" Elly ran for it as if she half expected the grey and white cat to be still in the seat before the controls. But it was empty.

Jim ran his hand across his forehead. Ever since they had gotten Tiro and Mer's message there had been one picture he had fought to keep out of his mind. And luckily he had had enough to plan and do to keep him from re-membering. But now he saw in a kind of ghostly way, spreading itself over the parked flyer, that horrible newspaper picture he had never told anyone he had ever seen. The pho-tograph of the smashed-up plane—the one Dad and Mom had been on—when they were killed.

He knew now that he had really believed deep inside that when they found the flyer it would be a wreck. Just as that other plane had been. But when he and Elly Mae hurried over to inspect it, they could discover no damage at all. It was just as if Tiro and Mer had set it down here as they would on the field back at the port.

Jim drew a deep breath of relief. All they had to do now was to find the Ka'ats. This was a small flyer; maybe it couldn't lift all four of them out. But the Ka'ats would be in the greatest danger. He and Elly had come into the city without trouble. They could send Tiro and Mer out in this flyer and then go back to their own.

Elly Mae stood still, both hands tight over

her ears, her eyes squinted shut. Jim knew without being told that she was trying to find Mer by mind-send. He sent out his own call, but he kept his eyes and ears open, too. They did not know how tricky the Hsi might have been when they built this place. There might be other guards beside the robots and Jim wanted to see danger coming if he could.

"Inside," Elly Mae nodded toward the tower. "And—"

Jim was already on the move. He slid into the seat of the flyer and studied the instrument board. Tiro wanted something, it was important. Not a weapon, at least none Jim could make out in the very hazy mind picture he could pick up now from the Ka'at scout. It seemed even more difficult than usual to understand just what Tiro was trying to tell him. The problem wasn't due to his own slow learning either; it was more like the way a television picture rippled back and forth on the screen when there was something wrong with the pick-up or when one of the tubes was weak.

Carefully, Jim began to put one finger at a time on the various levers and dials before him, hoping that Tiro could read his mind and give him a stronger hint as to what the Ka'at was so determined that he find. Tiro was desperate and afraid. Catching that fear scared Jim in turn. Since the beginning of this wild adventure, when they were still back on Earth, he had, he now realized, put a lot of trust in the Ka'at who could read minds and who was able to do so much that Jim's own kind had not yet learned, who came of a species that star voyaged about the time Jim's humankind had stopped living in caves and built the first tiny towns of mud bricks.

The fifth thing he touched, a dial which protruded farther from the surface of the board, brought a sharp mind agreement from Tiro. This was what was important. Jim crowded close to feel around the edge of the thing. It was about the size of half an orange, with a glassy, domed surface. On it there was a play of color, threads of light spiralling around and around.

He picked at the collar that held it to the board and all at once something, perhaps a catch he had not seen, gave way. It fell forward so unexpectedly that he had just time to catch it in his other hand before it thudded to the bottom of the cockpit. Now they had to find Tiro.

They had discovered but one door into the tower—the closed one. So they went to stand before that.

"There ain't so many of them tin can people out there now," Elly said.

With one hand on the closed door, Jim turned to the outer roadway. She was right. He saw a robot, or even two or three at a time, turn into one of the narrow alleyways and disappear.

All they had to do now was break through this door. There was no knob to turn. Even when they both gave all their strength to pushing, it did not move. There were no windows. What did they do now?

Elly kicked at the door. "Devil made it, seems like!" she sounded as if she were about to cry.

Jim was ready to agree with her. He was sure the Ka'ats were in terrible danger somewhere inside. But how were he and Elly going to blast through this solid material to get to them? That just could not be done.

What had Dad said—"Don't lose your temper when something doesn't work out the way you want it to. Try and think what you may be doing wrong or if there's some way better to try it."

Jim thought. There were different kinds of doors. Some were the ordinary ones with knobs and latches or keyholes, like the ones you saw in almost every house on Earth. Then there were those slatted ones Mom had in the bedrooms for the closets at home. They folded back like screens. But this certainly was not like that. There were no slats or divisions where it could be folded. Then there were doors at the supermarket that opened when you stepped on the floor in the right place, or crossed an invisible beam of light or something. Jim did not know just how they worked, only that they did—just seemed to open if you went towards them. Also, there were elevator doors which slide from one side to the other—

Doors which slid to one side!

"Elly," Jim turned to the girl, "you put your hands here—right on a level with mine. Now push! But don't push in, push sideways, like you want to push the door toward this wall—see!"

She was with him in a minute, her thin face filled with fierce determination. They pushed —nothing happened. Jim felt let down. It had seemed a good idea for a moment or two.

Then he had another thought; suppose

pushing was all right, but they had done it in the wrong direction? People, unless they were left handed, usually pushed from left to right. But suppose in this world that was reversed?

"Try again," he ordered, "only now the other way."

They pushed.

Somewhere there was a click, then a harsh grating, as if some machine did not want to obey. It did not do it easily, but the door *was* moving, toward the left!

It went so hard it set them puffing. But at last they had an opening wide enough to slip through. Jim took his small bag of supplies and wedged it between the door and the other side. He was sure that it couldn't shut all the way if he left that there.

Elly had already squeezed in and now he heard her impatient demand, "Come on! We've got to find Mer—before something bad happens. We just got to!"

7

The Prisoners

THE CHILDREN were in a big hall with many doors along each side. Not too far ahead was the beginning of a staircase that wound around and around until it disappeared through a hole in the ceiling. Elly ran straight for that. Jim was hardly a step behind her, the half-globe of flickering light held tightly against his chest. Both of them had picked up that mind-send at the same time. Somewhere above, the Ka'ats were in great danger.

The steps were covered with something soft like carpet, though to Jim that covering looked exactly like stone. Now they popped through the hole in the ceiling. Just one big room here, no hall or doors. Around most of the walls squatted boxlike things that Jim eyed warily—wondering if any were another kind of robot ready to come alive as they passed and throw out a clawed arm to catch them.

But the boxes remained quietly in place. Only across their fronts were lines of small squares, not much bigger than his thumbnail, and those *were* alive. At least with a soft, clicking purr they flashed lights on and off to make patterns which did not last long enough for him to really see.

Jim recognized them from a television special he had seen at school a year ago. These were computers! He looked around, waiting for one of the walking robots to come in and look for a spit out card, or else tear off some of a roll of paper one of the machines might stick out like a nasty tongue. But there was nothing like that. Just the boxes clucking quietly away.

"Come on!" Elly was already well up the next section of the circular stairs, heading for a second opening in the roof above. She had not even glanced at the computers.

But again she was right: the two Ka'ats they wanted were not here. So Jim hurried on. This time it seemed to him that the signals in his head sounded louder, if a thought could *be* louder. And, when they burst out on the next level, he discovered his guess had been right. Following the curve of the wall, set up on legs so as to bring their bases about waist level with the walking robots, were—cages! There was no mistaking the use of the wire netting-enclosed places. In one Tiro already crouched, his spine fur standing well on end, his ears flattened against his skull as he snarled defiance.

Just as the children arrived, one of the walking robots dealt expertly with Mer, as if handling a raging and frightened Ka'at was something it had done many times before. Grasping the spitting, clawing captive by the nape of the neck, the robot pushed Mer into another cage beside Tiro.

"No!" Elly screamed and jumped at the robot, pounding its metal body with both her fists. The machine paid no attention. Mer was in the cage, and the door slammed shut.

"Stop it, you—you old tin can!"

The robot was unmoved by either Elly's shrill cries or her attempt to grab hold of its nearest arm. Rather it shook her off, and she came flying back against Jim. Then the robot, unconcerned, turned purposefully to the other wall where there were two levers, lights winking brightly above both.

"They kill—" Tiro's thought tore into Jim's

mind with as much force as if the Ka'at had been able to reach out and rake claws across the boy's face. "Now they kill!"

Elly was screaming, running back to the cage that held Mer to pull vainly at the wire netting door.

"No use—" That was Tiro. Mer crouched to look straight into Elly's eyes as if even now she wanted to comfort the little girl.

Jim moved, getting to the wall before the robot. The levers were behind his shoulders. He faced the machine, still holding the half-globe, though that was certainly no weapon. But there was nothing else he could grab to fight with. Already the robot was reaching out, the boy was sure, to push him away so it could get at the levers.

"*NO!*" In his fear and hatred for the moving mass of metal Jim shouted. Not shrilly as Elly had, but deeper and heavier.

To the boy's amazement, the claw about to close on his shoulder stopped, only inches away. There was a queer humming sound from the robot, as if it was somehow either asking a question or perhaps protesting.

"Think 'no'—" Tiro's mind-send was very

clear. "Say your 'no' again. But into the force unit in your hand, and in a deeper voice if you can."

Jim could not understand the meaning of all this, but he was willing to try anything, anything at all. He cleared his throat and then held the half-globe out right in front of his lips. "NO!" he repeated, in as deep a voice as he could produce.

The robot shifted uneasily from one of its broad feet to the other. Those discs of light that completely surrounded its conical head flickered on and off, rather like those on the panels of the computer below. And that flashing grew faster and faster as the clawed arms snapped straight and fell to the robot's sides. Jim backed away until he could feel a lever poking him hard against a shoulder blade. He had kept this thing from pulling the lever, yes. But how had he done it, and if it started to move, how could he keep it from trying again? Could he smash up this robot if it really came for him? Of course, he could not! So what happened now? He mind-sent that question to Tiro with all the force he could summon.

"Open it! Jim, come and open the door!" Elly had apparently paid little attention to his stopping the robot. She was busy lacing her finger in the wire of the cage front and pulling, or pounding with her fist as hard as she could all around the edge of it.

"It cannot be opened now," Tiro's thought seemed to boom as if the big Ka'at could shout as loud as Elly. "It is locked by a force that keeps it shut."

"Then how are we going to get you out? And what do I do with him?"

Jim kept his place in front of the levers, but he leaned out a little so he could see Tiro better around the body of the robot. "Suppose I just tell him to let you go—"

"You cannot," Tiro returned. Elly was crying now, the tears running down her brown cheeks as Jim had only seen them once before, when Elly's Granny had died and she knew she was all alone in a world that had never been kind to her.

"But I stopped him from pulling that lever, or whatever he planned to do over here!" Jim protested. "And if I could do that, why can't I tell him to open the cages and then just go and jump off this tower or something while we get away!"

"The Ka'ats make their servants work

106

through thought. But the Hsi were different," Tiro returned. "When the Hsi began to fear the Ka'ats they did not allow mind-send to be built into their machines. These machines of the Hsi work by spoken command—and by what you hold in your hand—"

Jim glanced at the half-globe. "I don't understand; am I talking the same language as the Hsi then? Were—were they Earth people?" That he could hardly believe.

"No. But you thought 'no' as you spoke it. And what you hold was Hsi made. We use it only as a direction finder. The Hsi used it differently. They thought and spoke, and so made the meaning of what they thought control the machine."

"But then I *can* make it do what I say!"

"Not so. You could send the robot a short message like 'no.' But you cannot make it do more than that. Try if you wish."

Without a word she dropped the pack and they pushed with all their might until a cracklike opening was visible again. Jim thrust the pack back in.

"We got to have somethin' to eat. Mer and Tiro, too. We can push something through that old wire," Elly protested.

"You wait here!" Jim ordered her and stepped over the pack into the open. He stopped to stick the locator into the front of his half dried jump suit and then sped around the wall of the tower to reach the flyer. Jim grabbed at the cushions in the cockpit. There were two smaller ones for pilot and co-pilot, and a longer one for the passenger section.

Loaded down with these he went back and passed them endways to Elly Mae. When the cushions took the place of the pack, he watched for a long moment to be sure that, soft as they were, they would hold against the pressure of the door. Luckily, they did.

Then he followed Elly Mae up to the cage room again. The robot still stood, his head lights awhirl, his arms dangling. Elly hurried to open the pack and was pushing bits of food through the wire netting, first to Mer and then to Tiro. Jim brought out the locator.

Tiro had said it would grow brighter as it came near to any source of power. Jim balanced it on the palm of his hand and tried to think about the Hsi city. Somehow he was sure that this tower was its very center. All right—that meant it would hold everything the Hsi would want to keep safest. And the source of the power which protected the city would be the most important thing to them.

On Earth, furnaces, and sometimes generators, and things like that were kept in basements, weren't they? Did this tower have a basement? He could not be sure but he could go and look. Only to leave the robot just standing there—Tiro said it would have to be given another order to bring it to life again. But what if something in the city, say one of those computers below did flash it a new order? He had to make sure before he left that he wouldn't come back to find Tiro and Mer, and maybe even Elly, all dead.

Jim moved as close as he could to study the levers without touching them. How were they set in there? Ah! He felt the same excitement he had known before. There were just two screws—and he had the thin edge of the locator to use as a tool to loosen them.

Once more Jim held the half-globe close to his mouth. "Go downstairs," he commanded in as deep a voice as he could, trying to hold in mind at the same time the picture of the robot walking away towards the top of the curving stair.

On the head the lights flashed and flashed.

But the robot did not move. But if Tiro was right, then how—?

"Then how are we going to get you out?" he repeated his earlier question.

"There is no way out," Tiro mind-sent. "These cages have been used many times to destroy our kin. Once they are closed there is a power that holds them shut. And that power cannot be turned off. It you had not stopped it, that machine would have pulled one of the levers behind you, and Mer and I would have vanished into dust. We have many tales of this place—for the Hsi used such devices elsewhere before they came into this locked city and tried to forget that the rest of our world existed."

Jim swallowed. It was a nasty trap, about the worst he had ever seen. If they could not get Mer and Tiro out—why, maybe they would starve to death, or die of thirst! There had to be a way, there had to!

"Will this thing come on again?" he asked, studying the robot. He did not like those whirling lights around the head, but the rest of it seemed almost as if it were half turned off, what with its arms dangling loose that way.

Now a clanging sound replaced the hum he had heard earlier.

"Not until a new command is given—I think—," but Tiro did not sound too certain. "At least that is how our servants work, and basically they are alike."

Jim wondered if he dared trust what he was sure was a guess on the Ka'at scout's part. On the other hand, he could not just go on standing there forever either. He *had* to think of some way they could get those cages open. Maybe if he could find some tools—though he had never seen a tool kit in the flyers. Or—

His downward glance caught and held on one of the sawtoothed lower arm claws of the robot. It made him remember a can opener, and the cage was rather like a can. Now, if he could just twist that dangling arm off and—

"NO!" Tiro had been following his thoughts. "If you touch the wires of this cage with metal you will die, for the force will follow the metal into your own body."

Jim slipped out from behind the robot and went to stand before the cages of the Ka'ats. Elly Mae was whispering to Mer, who gave a purr in return. He hoped she would take it easy now until he got something figured out—

"There is no answer," Tiro mind-sent.

Jim shook his head. "There's got to be!" He was *not* going to give up so easily. Force, running through the wires, holding those doors shut—electricity? Could be, or something very like it. And what happens in a storm? He thought back on the night when they left their home world; during that storm all the lights and power went out halfway down the street. Electrical storms did that on Earth—blew the system. But what kind of a system would there be here? And if he did find the main switch, would he even recognize it?

Oh, there were a lot of things which might go wrong, but suddenly Jim felt very excited. If he could only find the main switch, or whatever the Hsi had used as a main switch!

"Yes!" Tiro's sharp thought startled Jim. "There is a chance, kin-cubling. To find it— that which you carry will aid you. The closer it comes to a source of power the more the light in it awakes. But where in this evil place you must search and for how long—"

"Just as long as it takes!" Jim promised.

Elly slipped past him, heading for the stair, and he swung towards her.

"Where do you think you're going?"

"I'm goin' to get that food—and some water—" she told him without looking around. Jim remembered the pack he had left wedged in the door to keep it open. But before he could warn her she was gone. He clattered down the stairs after her but she had already pulled it almost loose by the time he caught up with her. One last tug brought it into her hands. The door closed.

"Now you've done it!" Jim felt at that moment as if he could have slapped her.

"Done what, boy?" She sounded very snappish indeed.

"Let the door shut. If we turn off the power so Tiro and Mer can get out of the cages maybe we won't be able to get the door open again. Come on, help."

As he set to work Elly came to join him.

"What're you doing?"

"See these screws? I think if I can get them out we can take off this lever—both levers—and just take them away. Then if that old robot comes to life again it isn't going to find any way of killing anyone."

"That's smooth, boy. Then where do we go?"

"I'm going to hunt where the power comes

from," he informed her with the beginning of a frown.

"Not without me," she told him, a scowl growing as quickly as his frown. "That's my Mer there; no one is going to hurt her if I can help it. We go together—"

Jim shrugged. He had long ago learned that when Elly Mae spoke in that tone of voice she meant exactly what she said. The first of the screws fell out, to roll across the floor.

8

Death of A City

THE LEVERS, Jim thought as he weighed one in his hand, were rather like small, heavy clubs. He did not know how good a defense they might be against a robot who was not half turned off, but he felt a lot better with it in his hand. Elly Mae had grabbed up the other one, swinging it around as if she would like to bang it at once against the robot.

Jim went back to the cages.

"We're going to hunt for that switch, or whatever it is," he thought at Tiro and Mer. "And we'll be as quick as we can."

Elly Mae had dragged more of their provisions out of the pack and pushed some crumbling crackers and a small hunk of cheese at Jim.

For the first time he thought of what they had come into the city to find—food. But there was no time to go hunting now for any food machine. And if, as Tiro had said, the machines of the Hsi were meant only to answer to voice commands, discovering any would make no difference because they would not know the right words.

"You goin' stick around here all day?" Elly Mae sputtered through a nearly full mouth of cracker. "We gotta get Mer an' Tiro out. But how are we goin' to do that, huh?"

"Remember how the lights went out along the street back home. when it was raining?" Jim asked as he hurried after her. "That was 'cause the power failed. We've got to find a way to make it fail here. So we look."

As they scrambled down the stairs together, Elly Mae nodded.

"We never had no 'lectric lights, Granny an' me. But you did, so you ought to know what we're looking for. Where do we begin?"

"In the basement, if there is one here." Jim glanced warily at the twinkling lights of the computers as they passed through the second floor. At least there were no walking robots in sight. And with the levers safe in their hands, even if a robot did get back up to the cage room it certainly could not turn on the killing power.

They reached the lower hall with all the doors, Elly Mae nearly falling down the last three steps of the stairs in her hurry. There was, Jim saw now, a much narrower stair leading from the back of the one they had just descended, going even farther down.

Here it was dusky, but not so dark that they could not see the steps. They were nearly down when they heard the steady *tramp-tramp* of robot feet.

"Stop him—quick! Like you did before!" Elly Mae ordered.

But could he? Jim's hands felt slippery, like they always did when he was really afraid. He elbowed Elly Mae tight against the wall of the stairwell and fumbled for the globe.

"Keep quiet!" he whispered. "Maybe it won't even notice us."

They could see dimly the bulk of the marching robot. As far as Jim could see, it was exactly like the one up in the cage room. Except that the lights around its head were not flashing on and off so fast or so brightly.

Jim tried to hold his breath. His elbow dug into Elly Mae as a warning, and she was as quiet as the wall against which he had pressed her.

Thump-thunk–thump-thunk– The robot was at the foot of the stairs now. Then it was turning, raising one foot to set it exactly in the middle of the first step.

Jim licked his lips, brought the half-globe closer to his mouth. He must make his voice sound right, keep in his mind exactly what he wanted.

"NO!"

The robot had its foot right on the step. But it did not raise the second one. Instead, it made that humming noise the first had made, as if it were asking why. And the lights on its head were sparking faster and faster.

"Come on!" Jim pushed Elly Mae with his shoulder. But she did not need that encouragement. She was already squeezing past the stalled machine, her lever ready in her hand to hit at it if necessary.

Jim followed her. Then he glanced back. The blazing lights on the robot's head lit up the passage before them for several feet. However, it was making no move to turn and try to catch them. Only it would be better to get away from here as fast as they could.

Elly Mae was already running full speed. Jim could hardly see her any more, once she got out of the range of the lights on the robot's head. Now the boy raced after her.

There were no doors along this passage, just plain walls, and no side ways either. They burst through another opening at the end into a room as large as the computer section. In Jim's hand the energy locator suddenly blazed up like fire, though it held no heat he could feel.

There were huge boxes here, towering up, for they had come out on a balcony above a deep space. And there was another flight going down again into what seemed to Jim to be a very dark place. He started down one step at a time to meet that dark and found that the locator gave off enough light now to see at least three or four steps ahead. And he was listening as he went. There might be a whole army of walking robots holed up down here. Or even other kinds, even more dangerous to meet.

The stair seemed to be a very long one and when they at last came to the bottom step Jim put out his arm as a bar to keep Elly from running heedlessly into what might just be the worst danger they had faced so far.

Those boxlike things they had seen from above now towered over them, each nearly as

119

big as half of a house, or at least a garage. And the floor under their feet, as well as the boxes, gave off a slight shaking all the time.

"Watch out! We've got to keep watching out," Jim warned.

Elly Mae swung her lever.

"Don't need to tell me that, boy! This here's sure a scary place."

They kept close to the side of the nearest box, then made a dart across the small space which divided it from the next, and then the next. Jim watched the locator. It was growing brighter all the time. So much so that he gave his lever temporarily to Elly Mae and covered the locator with his hand for fear that something—or someone—might see it.

The place they explored was very wide. Jim counted boxes as they went, fearing that if they were able to do what they had come to do they might be lost later when they tried to get away again. Then he heard a small ghost of a laugh from Elly Mae.

"Look—" She held out a small lump of cheese, soft and rather grimy looking. "I'm marking these here old things," she thumped the lever against the box beside which they were crouched for that moment. "See—?" she

121

drew the lump of cheese down the smooth metal right above where the lever had hit.

Why had he not thought of that? Jim was mad at himself. But Elly Mae always did have at least some of the answers.

They came from the shadows of the last box and suddenly they were in the open. Not only in the open but in a glare of light bright enough to make their eyes smart so they had to blink before they could see at all. In the middle of the floor was a kind of well with a railing around it. The well was not too deep, but big enough so there was an open space about the length of Elly Mae's arm around a huge bubble. And the bubble was filled with a blazing fire—not just red and yellow as the fires the children knew, but with added tongues of green and blue, whirling around and around until Elly Mae caught at the railing.

"It makes my head dizzy to watch!" she complained. With one hand she clutched at her stomach. "I'm goin' to be sicker than if I ate a snake!"

The ball in Jim's hands lost its brilliance near this huge source of light. But it was bright enough for him to guess they had found what they were hunting. That colored fire burning in there was energy, like electricity maybe, light that one might see if a great big bulb was turned on.

But how did you turn this one off? Like Elly Mae, he discovered he felt sick if he tried to watch it closely. Slowly he edged completely around the well in the floor, one hand on the railing, the other cradling the locator. There were no levers, no control board, no buttons—nothing!

He felt more and more helpless. Somehow he had been sure that all he need do to rescue the Ka'ats was to find that place and just turn off the power. But how *did* you turn it off when there was just a big ball of light and nothing else?

Elly Mae stood up straight now. She swung one of the levers in either hand as she looked straight at Jim.

"Is this here that bad old thing that keeps Mer in the cage?"

"I think so."

"All right then. What are we waitin' for now? We just smash it then!"

"No!" shouted Jim. They did not know enough about that fire inside the big bubble.

What if it would explode, knocking over this whole building?

But Elly Mae wore her stubborn look and it was plain she was not going to listen to him. All that mattered was that Mer was in a cage and she was going to get her out. Before Jim could reach her, Elly Mae drew back her arm and threw the first of the two levers out at the fiery bubble, squinting her eyes against the glare as she did.

Jim heard the clang of the metal lever against the bubble. The second lever was already following the first.

"Throw it—" Elly Mae had raced around the section of the wall. Now, before Jim could fend her off, she grabbed the locator out of his hand and threw that, too.

There was a terrible blast of sound. Jim tried to cover his ears and saw Elly Mae crouched on her knees doing the same. He had expected to be burned up by flames shooting out of the broken bubble. His skin did feel all tingly and queer, and he saw Elly Mae's hair was standing straight up from her head. He was never sure later that he had not also seen sparks shooting away from her frizzy strands.

But—

They were in the dark. The light was gone. For a terrible minute or two Jim was afraid that he was blind. Then he realized that there was a very, very dim greyness.

Reaching out, he caught Elly Mae.

"Let's get out of here!" At least he meant to say that; he thought it, but he could not hear himself. And that scared him, too.

Somehow, feeling for Elly Mae's smears of cheese on the sides of the towering boxes, they staggered back to the foot of the stairs, clinging together. The humming, crackling feeling was gone. Jim shivered. This was like being near a big, dead, cold thing—

At the foot of the second stairs lay a tangle of twisted metal. The robot they had left on the bottom step had collapsed. It must be dead too, Jim thought wildly. He wanted nothing more than to get out of this place, as far from it as he could run. But there were Tiro and Mer.

Back they climbed. This time there were no lights along the computer machines, no quiet clucking or humming sounds. The room was dead and beginning to get very cold. The children hurried through it.

Just one more flight of stairs now. Somehow they scrambled up those. Here were the cages and over there lay another jumble of clawed arms and postlike legs where the other robot had fallen.

"Got to get out of here—" Now Jim could hear his voice again, though it sounded faint and far away somehow. But the cages were still tightly shut. Elly Mae was crying and pounding at the one holding Mer, but Jim went to Tiro's with a question.

"Is the force still in the door?" He shaped his thought as clearly as he could.

The big Ka'at seemed to be sniffing along the wire. "No, cubling. This is but metal now."

"Okay." Jim went over to the dead robot—he thought of it now as "dead." The boy pried and pulled until he got that arm with the heavy claws loose. He brought it back to the cage and, just as he had hoped, rubbing those along the wire could and did break through the strands. First Tiro and then Mer jumped to the floor.

Tiro lifted his head high as if he first was listening and then testing the air with his nose.

"The city is dead," he thought-sent. "Just like the Hsi who made it. But even dead it will have its uses—"

Jim sat down on the floor. He was tired; he was still shaky from the awful fear he had known when Elly Mae broke the bubble; he was thirsty and he was hungry. So—the city was dead—then let them get away as soon as they could. He—he hated this place! There was something about its plain, heavy buildings with no windows and their closed doors that made him feel as if he was in a cage just as the Ka'ats had been.

"Yes, we shall go, cubling," Tiro agreed. "But our Great Ones, they will send others. There must be much useful knowledge stored here. For to this place the Hsi brought all their records and their learning.

"You—," he rubbed his head against Jim's cheek in a caress he had never shown the boy before. Elly Mae, tears still wet on her face, was hugging Mer tightly as if she could never bear to let the Ka'at go again. "You have done very well, both of you, cublings. There were those among our Great Ones who feared that you would bring us only trouble. Instead, we shall have two more names to remember in our Calling of the Honor of the Ka'at— Kindarth proved himself Ka'at-kin in the long ago. Now you cublings have done likewise. It

may be that there has long been, for both our peoples, wrong and twisted thinking about who can be kin with whom. Kin-kind does not mean fur on one body, bare skin on another; it lies deep within one. I have claimed you, cubling, and Mer has claimed this other, and had we not so claimed you this trap of the Hsi would have gone on and on catching the unwary—a place of evil we had not the power to shun forever."

"We talk too much," Mer beamed a thought that was clearly impatient. "If it pleases the Great Ones to come here exploring later on, then let that be their choice. For me—I want the free air of our own places about us."

"Yes," Elly nodded. "I don't like this old city—it's bad."

They found their way back to the flyer. Crowded though it was with the four of them, and hardly able to rise above the tops of the city buildings, yet they took that way of escape. They found the other flyer parked where the children had left it. Tiro chose to ride with Jim, fascinated that the boy used the hand controls the Ka'ats had half forgotten.

"There is much we can learn one from the other," he told Jim as they rose into the air to follow the other flyer, already nearly out of sight. "And it will be a good learning, Ka'at-kin. I shall not speak again of you two as cub-lings, for what you have done this day makes you both true Ka'at-kin."

As Jim took off for the port he forgot all the impatience and hurt feelings that had brought him here. He even began to wonder how it would be to really explore the Hsi city now that its defenses were gone and the robots all safely dead. There was certainly a lot for a full Ka'at-kin—he was proud of that, knowing what it meant for Tiro to call him by that name—to do on Zimmorrah in the future.